Artist Girl's

Cambridge Daze

An experimental novel

Also by Judy Pokras

The Little e-Book of Raw Vegan Holiday Recipes
The Little Book of Raw Vegan Holiday Recipes
(Editor) *The Little e-Book of Raw Vegan*
Thanksgiving Recipes
by Great American Raw Chefs

Artist Girl's Cambridge Daze

An experimental novel

Judy Pokras

Drawings by Judy Pokras

First paperback edition, 2012

Artist Girl's Cambridge Daze / Judy Pokras

Drawings by Judy Pokras

Cover drawing by Judy Pokras

Cover photo by Judy Pokras

Grateful acknowledgement is made to the following for permission to reprint previously published material:

McGraw-Hill: One paragraph from *Culture Against Man* by Jules Henry (1965)

Facebook.com/CambridgeDaze

To my parents

Table of Contents

Artist Girl's
Cambridge Daze

A novella

Chapter 1

The French visitor who spent most of her time in the fishbowl living room thought the Artist Girl was inane. The French visitor was big, unfeminine and harsh. The Artist Girl was insecure and pretty. She was in a small room, standing on a blanket-covered metal wardrobe (which was on its side, bench-wise) to reach the curtainless curtain rod. She hadn't removed her shoes for the blanket's sake because she needed the height-boost to push a string tied to the curtain rod a few inches to the left. The string's other end was attached to a small rubber or plastic glow-in-the-dark ball. She had had a tangerine for breakfast after waking around 3 in the afternoon.

This room she affected her minuscule affects on was the one she lived in. It got virtually no sun, because of the blockage of the adjacent buildings and (during the only sun-allowing hour) because of shades, which knew no shades of gradation, from seven-eighths down to seven-eighths up, as they didn't roll. Thus the percentage of sun blockage combined with practicality to deem the eight-eighths down shade as allowing maximum privacy with minimum labor. In order to make a change in degree of upness or downness, one would have to:

1. Stand on the blanket-covered ex-wardrobe
2. Remove the top shade from its side slots
3. Hold the entire heavy shade high in the air, arms raised above head, and
4. Roll the shade by tiny turns of the small circumference roller
5. Then replace it, a bit easier than threading a needle, in its side slots.

She needed coffee and probably would also eat rice. The French visitor walked in circles in the living room, saying, "It's around here somewhere; is it here?" as she passed the closed door of the Artist Girl's room.

The Artist Girl was sitting on the blanket-covered wardrobe. She leaned against a large borrowed AM radio, which was part of a broken record-player. The combo wasn't large enough, though, to maintain its place with Artist Girl's back against it. The combo slid at unevenly spaced intervals when it absolutely couldn't fake strength anymore, like a guy trying not to breathe heavily while sitting next to an attractive girl in a dark movie theater.

She left her uncomfortable seat to get the coffee.

On finishing the coffee and rice, she returned to her room, having exchanged event reports with a fellow apartment dweller. She donated information on her current lukewarm job search. She received information from two fronts. The apartment mate would be moving to the mountains, the ski-mountains, to be a maid. A ski free six days maid. And an ex-apartment dweller gave Ski Maid the information that he'd become a bookie earning $500 a week. He had formerly been a graduate student in flute playing.

Ski Maid knocked on the door and invited Artist Girl to accompany her to a birthday party of someone the latter didn't know. Artist Girl was now sitting on the bed, leaning against the wall, which well took her weight without even a ghost of a slide.

Chapter 2

Artist Girl thought about the birthday party. "How stupid is it to go to a birthday party for someone you don't know? It is worse than eating sour balls when you know the gate blocking off your windpipe is broken. It is torture."

Artist Girl attended knowing that everyone at the party was well acquainted with everyone else. She knew only Ski Maid, who left a half hour after arriving, with a fabricated excuse. Loosely woven, even. Thus Artist Girl listened to a few hours of volleyballing conversation. The volleyball was the topic of schizophrenia. They tossed it back and forth while she seethed in tough silence. Soon she wouldn't be able to contain her overbearing imagination. The sieve she spoke through most of her speaking time anywhere was getting clogged with general air pollution. So even the fillers that were thin enough ordinarily to fit through the sieve holes, like "uh huh" and "of" and "the" and "oh" weren't able to get through. They collected like nicotine and tar do in the lungs. But she didn't cough. She drew a few more smiling ladies with overlong arms.

Artist Girl developed busman's holiday brand insomnia. She got business ideas at 4:30 and 5:15 a.m. She was thinking of marketing a spray can called Instant Recognition. It would sell well in Cambridge, Massachusetts, a town of brick sidewalks and 24-hour book stores and no spotlights. And anti-climaxes too.

"It comes out frazzled when you have to speak through a sieve."

Smiling lady with overlong arms

Chapter 3

Artist Girl took a vacation. Or did it take her? Its name was "going home for Thanksgiving" but she stayed about two weeks longer. Her stay was as full of textural riches as a Superman comic book. Its highlight was the audacity she unleashed to record the names of the most quirky males she could find in the town's high school yearbook, the one coinciding with her graduation year. (This town where her family lived was not the one in which she had gone to high school.) She selected, as was in keeping with her culture--the culture of her adolescence and childhood, if not now--the best guy, and drew an asterisk next to his name.

She returned to her small room in Cambridge and didn't feel particularly emerged from the comic book dimensionality. More highlights, more repetitions. She wrote a letter to a back home friend, relating the back home highlight, by way of excitement. (She hadn't been able to reach the friend by phone.)

A guy who lived around the corner in Cambridge dropped by to exhibit his latest piece of writing. Artist Girl thought he had a conveyor belt sort of sensitivity. Styles, words, rolled out of him with the effortlessness of a Dugan's lemon pie on its way to a meringue. She lied to him after he observed her inclusion/transfusion of people she knew into "material" for her stories. She lied as she told him she could only write of those who seemed not as people to her. Of those who might as well have been lamps or chairs. "I could never write of *you*," she said soberly. Even believing herself.

Thus betraying her friends, she self-exiled. To the quixotic occupation of traveling alone to free jazz concerts and free movies, not able to ignore bits of "material" she would very much like to have dematerialized into those she knew. This solitary asceticism did her no good. She began reflecting on her state of sensitivity. "I'm so sensitive, I'd feel an atom shitting on me." Solipsistic, she became a

cheap vaudeville comedian as she spoke to herself.
"Spending money? Extravagance for me is going
into Woolworth's and buying two types of
envelopes--airmail and regular."

.

Chapter 4

Waking and lifting/kicking with the hands the broken window shade to see if it was at least a blue sky. It was, with a wind. Piano music through the floor above was oblivious to her little radio. Two reminders stuck in a sitting position with tape to the top of the radio were not polite enough to bow or curtsy each time the typewriter carriage rode by. Thus they got a paper beating. Artist Girl, half-sleeping, bore the object details without a fizzle. She waited for the right awake moment to plunge her into the kitchen, then to drink a coffee, thus to be able to enter people-detail territory, infinitely more fascinating.

Last night at a lecture, the fine photographer said many honest and humble things. His photographs were combinations of two or more negatives with perhaps a lettuce leaf thrown in. One bunch was grouped on the theme "hands." He liked juxtaposing hands with people. He said, "People ask me why I use hands as an image so frequently. I don't really

know. I guess because they're so convenient;
they're right there at the end of the wrist. And hands
touch. I'm very concerned with relationships."

Artist Girl was thinking he was saying too much.
She wanted him not to talk anymore. But he did. He
showed a group of images containing a person
superimposed on a rock. "Sometimes," he said, "a
person is prevented by no failing of his own from
doing what he would want to. Things like skin
color, financial situation, intellectual capacity" —he
didn't mention gender—"keep a person from
succeeding. And sometimes I feel trapped like that.
Like when I was at that meeting of important
photographers in Chicago and there was no
meaningful conversation. There we all were,
sensitive people, and no one was saying anything
beyond polite conversation."

Artist Girl wondered how the rest of the audience
was taking his comments.

He continued: "I hate the idea of being considered a
teacher. I tell students that I'm happy to be able to

tell them how I've achieved certain results by techniques. Any technical assistance I can offer is theirs. But as far as being able to tell them anything about life, I want them to understand that I'm still floundering for answers. I could easily give a smooth talk on photography, with all the proper comments, and you'd all go away from the lecture saying, 'Oh that Jerry Uelsmann is all right. He's got it all together.' But I haven't got it all together at all."

Ho, that's just how Artist Girl felt when people looked at her drawings, marveling at her "talent." What a lot of rot it was, anyway. It separated her more than any beneficial thing it might do, by bringing her the left-handed compliment of awe/praise/fear. Yes. That man had a lot of courage to stand in front of all those pretty people and say what he did. Or maybe it wasn't courage. Maybe he'd gone so far, he'd had to. Like John Lennon in his famous *Rolling Stone* interviews.

After the lecture, which was unduly straining-- Artist Girl being forced by a dirty floor and lack of seats to stand for an hour and three quarters--she went to a basement bar with tables, accompanying her escort, a bumbling uptight boy. He was nice, exactly as is the word "nice." Not exactly the word one could apply to something stunning and magnificent. This was the sixth time he'd taken her out in eight or ten weeks. He reminded her of one of Santa's elves due to his beady though not sinister eyes and his diminution with her. Poor shy subordinate. When he tried to kiss her goodnight, she decided it was time to terminate their rounds. He didn't have any ego to worry about shattering.

Chapter 5

"Obediently he followed her into the street which was congested by the traffic and office workers scurrying to lunch." Artist Girl read that sentence around five time before she realized she was not going on, as is the natural progression, to the one after it. It was in the book on her lap, the book she was reading, *The Journal of Albion Moonlight* by Kenneth Patchen.

Earlier that day she was in New York City, at a job interview. The portraits of eight former company presidents were on the wall opposite the reception desk. None of them did not wear a tie. Six wore glasses. Looking at the interviewer's head, one would think he'd have a sunken consumptive chest. Instead it was as if stuffed with bits of rag and old newspaper. Puffed out in an unnatural way. He pronounced his "L"s like "GL"s.

Artist Girl looked into his eyes, in her scheme of pretending sincere interest WITH enthusiasm, in case she decided to take the job. The interview lasted one hour. It was in the audio-visual room of an accounting firm. She almost left her umbrella behind.

"For an intelligent girl, you have some funny ideas," her father said, in answer to her complaint that accountants are boring and conservative and unimaginative.

She walked out of the accounting company hating offices more than ever, more, almost, than when she had had to work in them in her trying past.

She wrote a resume to send to the accounting
company:

Artist Girl

Formal education:
Pratt Institute. Three years. Art major
London Film School. One year. Filmmaking

Jobs:
These, due to overabundance, will be separated into
subject categories to facilitate quick judgment on
part of overseers. (The hirers, the sizers up.) For a
chronological picture, see attached sheet.

Art-related:
Freelance illustrator for Orson Welles Film School,
Cambridge, Massachusetts
Cover illustrator and designer for Spiro Agnew
comedy album
Freelance illustrator for Peace News, London,
England

Freelance illustrator for Christmas cards, NYC

Logo designer (corporate identity) for the Sellar

Boutique, Livingston, NJ

Film-related:

Assistant film editor, WGBH, Allston,

Massachusetts, one month

Assistant film editor, Psychology Today film, NYC,

one month

Production assistant, Director's Studio, NYC, one

month

Receptionist, PDR Productions (film editing

company), NYC, three months

Picture editor, TVC VideoRecord (photoscript and

kinescope company), NYC, three months

Resume, continued

Statement:

My jobs did not last long because I was too ambitious and too lacking in the patience required to remain in an unsatisfying job. In short, my tasks were always too menial mechanical rather than creative. I had the fortitude not to quit, but worked slowly to compensate for my lack of enthusiasm so that the quality of my work would not suffer. In at least two jobs there were complaints of slowness. This was due to my forced effort at a job beneath my qualifications, abilities.

I'm writing this in complete honesty, if perhaps a stubborn, persistent, naive idealism. Thus, I tell you I can take no more anguish as I have encountered in my search for meaningful, satisfying work. I am tired of pretending to be enthused when, in fact, I am not. I am ready to take a job having permanence. This is because I think there is enough to interest me here. (LIE!) I can learn accounting while helping make up the slide presentations. I hope you'll agree with my decisions.

Artist Girl read the resume to her parents.

"It looks like you don't want the job, then," said her father.

Chapter 6

Eleven apartments, 31 jobs and 200 dates or escorts in four years. Artist Girl decided it was time for some stability. But being unfamiliar with it, she didn't know how to find some. You don't, one doesn't, she thought, put an ad in a financial-security-conscious newspaper like the *West Essex Tribune* under Positions Wanted saying, "Young girl, capable yet talented, desires a modicum of stability. Will send resume."

She was back to mistaking spiral notebook page holes for black ink spots on her hands and fingernails--admittedly after an experience with a leaking pen and minus her contact lenses. "Ah, the blurs, the generalizations, the errors of perception."

Chapter 7

Artist Girl laughed to herself despite the ever intensifying paranoid expression on her face as she stood in the third isle from the right as you face the rear of Purity Supreme Supermarket, looking at the cookies. She laughed in disbelief at the attention she gave the cookies: the amount of deliberation she was going through in the process of deciding which box to buy, if indeed she was to permit herself this luxury. Luxury was taunting her to buy the rich in ingredients Pepperidge Farm small pack, which would leave her in a contrary-from-the-first-adjective-describing-the-cookies state. But she sensed that Luxury, in its ephemeralness, would lose out to old tough stanchion Economy. Now the question became: Will it be crackers, which bow favorably to economy, in that they're individually less appealing to the tongue than their sweeter relatives, thus will last longer? Or will it be cookies, which have more charm than character?

Interspersed with this debate was the pressurized cabin of Rushing Others. How can I leisurely stand here when the business at hand is grabbing, paying for and carrying the bundle home, in the race to consume? How dare I indulge my logic in public?

At some point herein, her "newness rule" demanded attention. And thus Artist Girl had to weigh the value of each shelved item not only for its taste and economy relative to her hunger's needs, but according to the rule that says "You must not buy any item you've bought before." Oh, she made damn sure she had enough on her mind so she couldn't possibly think more than once every three minutes of how there might be a possible new male friend rolling his shopping cart past any time now.

Chapter 8

She allowed herself brewing space, she realized.
But not brewing time. She allowed fragmentary
inspirations to go unrecorded and unsubsidized. A
sentence would come into her awareness and she
would accept a smile as its only reward. She was
lying on her low bed. The dark room was aided by
no lights of Artist Girl's admission. She became
aware, by and by, of the phrase "allowed herself
brewing space." "It must be something I've written
before," she thought. It sounded so familiar. "But
what about brewing TIME? I cannot reconcile the
acceptance of one and the ignorance of the other."
Artist Girl thought further. "Why can I not give this
psyche the freedom from ticking, from day-names
that it needs, that it demands?"

She found it complex to continue. There was the
choice of the fine music on the radio as
accompaniment to her thought process. But it was

too strong, too distracting. Its function was really as cover-up for the other choice, the choice of the louder, crude music seeping through the door from the fishbowl living room. There was no silent ground here. And a request, i.e. complaint, in favor of living room silence would be unjustified, probably, this weekend afternoon.

This led her to thoughts of martyrdom. "I rationalize every disturbance out of the complaint-behavior it might most healthily merit." The seven co-residents of the apartment were throwing the mud at Artist Girl for her incomplete paper bag structure's obtrusion of the communal living room space. "We can't walk by it," they complained. "It's impractical," they tried to reason. Artist Girl was building it out of a uniformity of supermarket shopping bags. She stapled them at their mouths, connecting all the individual bag walls into one beehive-like wall. This she would build until it had reached ceiling-to-floor proportions, and then she would work on its width, eventually connecting the growing wall with itself, to form a cylinder of paper bags around an empty center.

Soon, surely, the most vile apartment resident would dismantle the incomplete structure, relegating the nearly glorified shopping bags to garbage status. Artist Girl would never impose herself so, on others. She rather seethed alone, hoping the rage would add texture to her art. She was thinking the bag structure was an homage to a long ago art school roommate and friend who had made one of these paper bag structures in their dorm apartment. Homage, taken from the French "homme" was a masculine word. It would have been equated with the English man-age, as homme equals man. And was there a French word "femage"? Not.

Chapter 9

The extreme wind catapulted Artist Girl's mood.
The energy of it. She arrived at a friend's
apartment.

As she wrote, Moby the orange cat sat on the page
purring without even a meow or a hello of
provocation from Artist Girl. Moby rubbed her nose
in Artist Girl's face and against her pen as she tried
to write. Artist Girl thought a lunchtime chopped
liver sandwich was making her sick. She felt the
sandwich plus the extreme wind outside the
apartment as an invisible chariot of horses whose
rider, leader, drove them away from her, behind her,
their reins attached to her eye sockets and jaws.
"The cat sits on my lap," she wrote, "Purring so
loud, I'd be embarrassed if I were it."

Artist Girl told her friend Bob about the song she
once wrote for Milo cat in London. Bob pretended

to go back to reading his book. He read the same sentence over and over, not even realizing he was not reading his book.

A bit later, Artist Girl, Bob and the other three friends were smoking grass. After a smoking while, Bob yelled, "Ow...what the hell...OW!" And they all noticed some ashes on his lap.

Chapter 10

Wilhelmina lived in a rice paddy. She was a lazy one, though, thus did none of the work associated with such. She watched those who worked. Watched them as they stomped on it with their feet. Watched them clean their fingernails as they sat in her cell visiting her. She watched them watch her and she made little clicking sounds in her imagination. Metronoming their duration. Five clicks for John. Fifty-one clicks for Helga-Marie. Seventeen clicks for Lewison. Clicking off. Off, for, in her concern to make an accurate click-count, she heard not much of what they said. She heard a bit here and some there and on and on. Like falling asleep and waking up and falling asleep and waking up and falling asleep and waking up while watching Godard's movie "Alphaville." She baked a fragrant pie and had not the nerve to reserve it for herself. She easily let her visitors nibble it away. What is the good of food anyway, she knew.

Chapter 11

There was once a girl who had a little curl. Right in the middle of her forehead. And when she was down, she was very, very down. And when she was down, she was horrid. That came into Artist Girl's head as she sat watching people walking in and out of the great high-ceilinged lobby of MIT's main building. She sat extremely angry. So angry that nothing would help her get rid of her anger except perhaps two things she was too inhibited to do: scream, and jump from a balcony to land in a splutter on the floor, with no more unassuageable anger. No more nineteen-year-old horny boys collecting around her as if she were their queen bee. No more nineteen-year-old girlfriend telling her she kept herself too attractive, nineteen-year-old girlfriend who always wore a hole-in-the-arm cardigan and who had scratched with a knife 20 lines into the skin of her own left hand out of anger. No more jobs to have to look for, humiliating

minimum-wage jobs, when she'd made three times
as much, previously. No more filmmaking
ambitions, impossible to fulfill. No more walking,
talking in a frenzied state, Cambridge acquaintances
seeing her as some kind of unmotivated dunce who
can't make a decision.

If she didn't know herself better, she'd be afraid to
sit with such a far down to the ground view. It was
probably 20 feet down from this purple carpeted
balcony.

All she needed--really needed--were two things: a
satisfying employment of her talents in exchange
for a living wage, and a fine man to laugh with. In
that order. And never were the possibilities so far
from being actualized. Now, when she knew she
had the requisite talents, charms.

She took a deep breath. And another. Nothing. She
heard an electric saw, she heard airplane sounds,
she heard people's voices muffled AND sharp.

She felt pressured. There was something--some

chemical, she supposed--inside her, forcing her to affect some change in her circumstances, in her environment, in her activity, that would overcome this telltale always-mood of down.

She would go back to her apartment and cloister herself in her room, but for the ever-intruding well-intentioned nineteen year olds who paid her visits as they would their shrine. No, there was nowhere to go. If only she were free to scream. Ah, but even primal therapy cost money. Money she didn't even have for food.

And, depressed and enraged as she was, she still maintained enough concern for others that she could not scream in any public or private place. Why alarm them?

People go insane for the simplest reasons, she thought. In my case, it's either my chemicals or not being able to find a suitable employment or fine-man. How simple and how impossible.

Oh to be running running running along the beach

in some warm climate. Oh to be a stallion or an eagle.

The electric saw noise was soothing. She just rode with the constant noise.

She remembered how, when she lived in London, she would paint a surface of a chair or bookcase red when she was feeling down. Some walls of her lightless room were already red, though, and she disliked the room too much, for its lack of light, to want to do anything visual to distract her feeling of down.

She could go to her room and sleep. But in her state, she was too afraid she wouldn't want to wake up.

And then, how long could she sit here, on this balcony, 20 feet above the lobby of MIT's main building? Other times, she might take herself to a movie, buy her way out of the down as a temporary distraction. But with only four dollars left in the bank, it was foolish to consider throwing three dollars of it to some movie that would be over too soon. And would leave her pining and hungry.

Why was she painting herself into a corner, she wondered. As if she sat there, writing less than Beckett could, until some charming fine-man would run up to her in a white horse costume and whisper that line from Ionesco's *The Bald Soprano*, "Elizabeth! I have found you at last!" Oh, but if that were even faintly possible at Pratt, for her 18-year-old self, MIT, the least romantic of schools, would not provide such for the over-Romanticism of her 24-year-old self.

Now the scraping of someone's shoes against the marble provided a momentary relief, the fact that someone didn't compromise with the ground by lifting their feet, but slid them along lazily, defiantly. Here was a positive sign. She heard more of it. Was it simply that she wanted to pick up on something, and that was there for her convenience, for her need?

It was comfortable on the balcony. She'd needed a refuge for some long time. She had none in this town. The Cambridge library was too far away. And it closed too early.

She leaned her head into the beautiful blonde sheep curls of her coat. She loved her coat. She hated for anyone else to sit on it, to lie on it. It was too much a part of her.

That reminded her of Milo the Siamese cat who used to visit her in London. Milo lived downstairs and belonged to a girl who lived with Artist Girl's love. (No one realized he was Artist Girl's love, though. They all thought he was just one of many in Artist Girl's collection. Even Artist Girl didn't know until it was too late. But she did know at the time Milo would visit her.) Milo would stare into Artist Girl's eyes, as if the cat could feel all of her despair. And Milo would purr and purr.

The few times Artist Girl encountered Milo *downstairs*, Milo wouldn't purr at all.

She missed Milo a lot. She used to put M. Balmain perfume on Milo. It smelled like lemon candy. She indirectly heard that it made the cat's owner very angry. But Milo liked the perfume. That was all that mattered.

She wrote a song that ended with: "Milo, Milo, take me for a ride on your motorcycle. I've seen you dashing through the streets of London and would like to go, too."

Artist Girl looked up from her writing and saw the nice back of a guy. He walked out the door of the lobby.

No, Artist Girl, you mustn't, you mustn't. You mustn't fall into that, or anything. If you are going down, you must jump. You mustn't fall. It must be a deliberate action. You must decide and then act. No more observing, pining and then falling down, DOWN.

She had a sudden craving to hear Tim Buckley's first two albums, especially the song "Pleasant Street" with its lyrics "You see, you hear, you fall down, down, down..."

She remembered one time at Pratt when she had a sudden craving to hear Peter Pan singing "I Won't Grow Up" and "I Gotta Crow." She had put up a sign announcing her desire to hear it. And some anonymous student brought the record to her dorm when she was out. In appreciation, she baked a cake for him as a thank you gesture and brought it along when she went to return the record. The anonymous student wasn't home. Upon seeing she had brought a cake, his roommate said, "Thanks. Put it in the kitchen. He got another one today." It turned out to be the anonymous guy's birthday.

"Today is Valentine's Day," Artist Girl wrote. "And I am wearing a red top and red socks. And I got no mail. And I am unbalanced. And unhappy. And I woke up this afternoon to, among other songs, 'I can't get no satisfaction' by the Stones. And I remember thinking, in my half-awake state, how perfect that song IS! And now I am thinking, 'Hmmm, I wonder how much longer that will be my perfect song. I hope not forever. I don't know if a person can be that strong. To take it forever.' "

Chapter 12

"...oh, the chapped fugues," she continued. She was walking from work to pleasure. She swallowed after she spoke. The branches she was eating stuck in her throat. It was winter, they had no foliage, they were sharp and thin and they didn't slide down. She had a cold. The sniff that she swallowed didn't wash down the branches. Her room being crowded with pursuing-people, she escaped to the vacant library of an art college.

She wasn't affecting a perfect balance. She wasn't directing her own days, let alone films. Who was she fooling? She was fooling herself. She did it almost very well. The lists she wrote out. The lines of things to do left on the page, facing out, not even held in place with a cross-out-line. She wasn't fooling herself very well.

She either had to accept the lack of heroes in the

world or she had to be such a played-to-the-hilt
heroine that she would be too occupied to notice the
lack. And such occupation was a shrifty shrew.
Damn greasy pig of an aspiration. Aspirate. Exhale.

She exhaled too much. Far out of proportion to her
inhale. Thus she appeared sultry. She of course had
acquaintances who did the opposite. They had no
exhale, or not much of one. They appeared fat and
complacent. And wheezed not a little. They could
spit, too, which they did, on her drawings. She
misinterpreted such as disdain. Actually, it was fear.
They hoped to rub out some of her strange
perceptions by bleeding the lines on a page. What
hopes THEY had, those who called HER
unrealistic!

Chapter 13

Her sense of the other was overdone. She boarded the train. The no-smoking car had maroon upholstered seats, which she found an unexpected pleasure, having a preference for blued reds. Another unhoped for pleasure was in the relative emptiness of the car. No families with nagging parents and rebellious children. No overabundance of students. A few people, but mostly empty maroon seats. She glowed at this opportunity for thinking. How wonderful it was to look out the window--at the sun and shadows, the pure visuals outside the train, and think. And there was also her heightened appreciation in that she had to record it all so quickly, as the train's motion allowed for no meditation on any objects, only momentary passing pleasure. Oh, the jumping-off points for her imagination. A lawn's row of burlap-covered bushes (protection against the frost) became a line of Halloween or bandit ghosts. And then further

visual stimuli quickly washed over the costume
image.

As she boarded the train and discovered the nice
emptiness, she knew it would be taken from her,
this thought-pleasure, as soon as people sat in any
line of her vision. Their presence would make
demands on her attention. She'd not be able to
ignore them in favor of the passing landscapes.
She'd without an effort be thinking on their stories,
or skeletal formations thereof. What does this fat
man do for a living? Why is he going south? What
about this pleasant-faced young guy behind me?
Why is he sitting in that seat? He doesn't have
much window and there are obviously better
window seats in other parts of this car. Why is he
reading? To alleviate any boredom he imagines
he'll encounter on this five hour train? Or because
he loves the book without reservation? (How
indeed, rare.) Or because he is a student and the
book is required reading? Has a friend
recommended it to him? Is he very conscious of the
girl sitting across the aisle from him wearing a
skirt? Is he in a foggy mood? (He sniffs

occasionally.)

She was slightly upset that people's presence stole
her from herself, so. Other people didn't seem to be
so affected by people's presence. The young guy
behind her still read. The girl in the skirt still read.
Artist Girl was not still looking out the window. For
a time, the passing visuals had been such a boost to
her imagination (which had been too long confined
to an art supply store where she worked for rent
money) that she hesitated to leave her seat to buy
coffee from the two-cars-away food car, for fear
that she would miss some beautiful thoughts
inspired by the scenery, which, though plotless, held
her attention as rigidly as any movie she didn't want
to miss part of to buy popcorn.

When she did decide to journey two cars to the rear,
the sight of a crowded car took her away still further
than those few proximate people did in the maroon
seat car.

There was a good-looking blonde guy to be
accounted for. (What magazine was he reading? Did

he like himself enough to have the aggression
necessary to attempt to meet her?) There was the
long-haired nine year old, listening to the earphone
of a tape recorder.

"What are you taping?" she asked him.

"I'm not taping, I'm listening," he said.

"Music?" she asked.

"No, it's a science report."

She thought, how lucky he is to have access to a
tape recorder at his age. She was jealous of his
opportunity, which she had missed. And she
couldn't help but think, I'd like to know him when
he is my age. Or, where are the guys now who were
this kid when I was seven or eight or nine?

Chapter 14

Artist Girl, seeing how her days are blending together and forming a rapidly soluble quicksand bog, decides to keep a journal or diary (not knowing the difference between the two) in hopes of finding an order, an incline in the graph of her manic-depressiveness.

TUESDAY

S'morning, reported to work after almost a week of absence. Boss wasn't too delighted with my insouciance. "Why," he said meekly (I mock), "didn't you call yesterday if you weren't coming in? You said you'd be back yesterday." I was as blandly agreeable as one would imagine a mole or a groundhog to be. I was also expressionless. Not even a tatter of sweet remorse on my eyes or my mouth.

And so it was that the boss handed me my last

paycheck, $32.35 for two or three days. Before nearly prancing (in a lack of being able to contain my expressiveness) out, I showed a fine, true paragraph to Elaine, the office worker, and to Jake, the young accountant. Surprisingly, the paragraph produced a smile and a "My!" from Jake. Jake seems to be a woman-hating mouse man, so short and thin, his only glory is in his sarcasm and lack of receptivity to my efforts at friendliness and flirting.

The paragraph was from a paperback called "Culture Against Man" by Jules Henry:

In our own culture the outstanding characteristic of promotable executives is drive. It is no problem at all to locate jobs requiring an orientation toward achievement, competition, profit, and mobility or even toward a higher standard of living. But it is difficult to find one requiring outstanding capacity for love, kindness, quietness, contentment, fun, frankness, and simplicity. If you are propelled by drives, the culture offers innumerable opportunities for you; but if you are moved mostly by values, you really have to search, and if you do find a job in which you can live by values, the pay and prestige are usually low. Thus, the institutional supports-- the organizations that help the expression of drives --are everywhere around us, while we must search hard to find institutions other than the family which are dedicated to values.

Chapter 15

Saturday.

Last night it was warm in here, unreasonably. So I turned the 65 degree thermostat down to 60 degrees. Woke up three minutes ago by a phone ring into an 85 degree room. What is doing this, then?

Had a dream that I was working in some sort of clothing outlet/store or depot. Was matching orders for white-on-red silk polka dot blouses. Sleeveless. Why the hell am I dreaming of clothes?

Wrote a letter to London Dave last night around 3 a.m. It put me in a good, positive energy mood! Today I am less enthusiastic about sending it. To send it would be insanely magnanimous and magnanimously insane! I think I am both of these. This moistureless room heat is dementing my already dehydrated mind. How good it would be to start every day with a loud scream. I think that would be more helpful than that ostensibly 100 percent minimum daily requirement cereal, "19."

I look at my 4 a.m. prepared list of active things to do and find it to be contrived and bursting with passivity, as if I had written it in day-glo ink, its only dynamism potential being the jumping-off-the-page power of its paint. A A A A A A H H H H H H H H H H H

Saturday, continued

I mailed the letter. I wasn't going to, but a new apartment mate, on hearing my last name, laughed at its Russian original. "Why are you laughing," I asked.

"I know some Russian," he answered.

"What does it mean?" I asked.

He said, "Well, it is hard to translate, to explain. Beautiful something..."

"I heard it means pretty flower," I said.

"Pretty flower?" He didn't seem to know.

I bought stamps, licked them and stuck them on their respective envelopes (a letter home and a letter to the missing hole-in-the-sweater friend) and walked towards the post office, still weighing doubts. I saw a mailbox closer than the post office. Before I got close enough to it to examine the collection times posted on the box, when I was five steps away, a big, wrinkled-faced bald man opened the letter drop and smiled. "I saw you coming," he said. I lost grip of my doubts at that point. He made the final decision. And my hand deposited the three envelopes, the doubtful, insanely magnanimous letter among them.

Back to the apartment. A discussion followed at the kitchen table, in which the new apartment mate increased my guilt about lying around and thinking while doing nothing.

I left with a sketchbook heading towards the library, a mile's walk. I decided to take a detour to the pet shop, decided while walking, my eyes tearing behind their contact lenses, from the wind or just the dirty still air.

In the pet shop, I visited the monkey. His mood seemed to coincide with mine. He wasn't being very friendly or flirty--or happy, a prerequisite for the other two. Poor caged bundle of intensity. I tried drawing him for a while. That was unsatisfactory. The sun through the window heated the indoor air to something approximating this afternoon's waking temperature in my room. The monkey moved too often to help my drawings. But I didn't blame him. I just wished he lived with me, somewhere in a sunny room with a view and no temperature problems and a radio. Oh, comfort. Oh, the ugliness of the part of the city my room happens to be in.

I showed the monkey my attempts at remembering him on the page. He hardly noticed. And I got to the library in time to reserve Norma Meacock's novel *Thinking Girl*. And to borrow a copy of Virginia

Woolf's *Three Guineas*.

I walked home, my eyes tearing for a mile, and practically collapsed on my bed. I crashed into oblivion, feeling not the slightest bit of energy or motivation to do anything else. I tried thinking of the letter I mailed to London Dave, but he probably isn't even at the address I sent it to, so that didn't spark me any.

I feel like I have mono. I feel like a shadow or a puppet whose strings are not being worked. I don't even feel crucified or caged anymore. Just lifeless, without muscle-power or ability to want to live.

London Dave and Artist Girl

Chapter 16

Artist Girl gave up her journal idea. She didn't feel
that being a subjective recorder would do her any
good. She and a friend had Sunday breakfast in a
bagel deli in Boston. They ate their fried kipper
with onions, their chopped liver salad platter. They
saw Joey, a high school acquaintance of Artist
Girl's, not seen since high school days, a
coincidence. They exited, not, as they well
expected, buoyed by the lush breakfast. Artist Girl
tried to perk her friend's sagging mien. "Let's
pretend we're tourists and just arrived in Boston!"
She added an extra exclamation mark. It didn't help.
The friend allowed herself, though, to be sucked
into the huge adjacent library. Once there, she
admitted to a fog, and ran out in despair.

Artist Girl tried the periodic literature room, to feel
more connected with now. Magazines rather than
books, this time. The shelves offered her nothing

more germane than the *Partisan Revue*. And she'd
never gotten to it before. Inside it, a fine identity
story. A female writing about a male, a famous
author she'd been acquainted with. How she hated
him for his fame and for the arrogance she saw in
him. She decided by the end of the story that the
arrogance was her projection.

Artist Girl was delighted with the story. It was not
til she'd finished it and looked up, into the room,
that she realized how--rarity indeed--she'd been
totally engrossed in the story. No looking up to note
the comers and goers. No noticing the good-looking
males--whether there *were* any.

In the looking up, she noticed a guy sitting at the
other side of the window seat she occupied. He was
accompanied by an envelope which bore the name
of the local counter culture newspaper's cartoonist.
(In fact, once a person looking at Artist Girl's
portfolio had compared her drawings to his, but she
didn't agree.) She looked back into the *Revue*.
(Backing into a critical article praising Norman
Mailer.) But she decided she had to speak to this

cartoonist guy. And she did. He was very pleasant, easy (in her disjointed state) to talk with.

Chapter 17

Artist Girl sat at a table in a coffee house. She was drinking coffee and planning on gazing out the huge window. A couple in their late thirties sat down at the table and blocked her view. The man had a lowish mealy melodic voice. It projected his overconfidence. His cockiness was set off by the casually attractive woman's flirtatiousness. They were perhaps co-workers having an affair. It was still in the exciting stages, something Artist Girl couldn't imagine experiencing ever again. She envied their insouciance and felt like a spy listening to their conversation. Perhaps, probably, she was the inspiring force, the silent, unrecognized third. They left too soon. The discomfort they inspired in her was replaced with emptiness when they left. And Artist Girl was forced back on her own situation.

The main character meets an acquaintance

Artist Girl rolled past the drugstore, past the African specialty gift shop towards the corner, onto the next block, still hurrying, the celluloid ribbons flopping from her shoulders, their 35-millimeter sections broadcasting small colored prints on the pavement.

She left traces of her image on the eyes of people who lined the sidewalk, quick traces moving across from left eye to right eye. Those whose eyes were touched had no control of duration of image; she was soon gone.

The end point of her journey was pushed back by an acquaintance whose figure jumped visually from one eighth to one half of an inch in her eye frame within a second. He, too, was quick-paced. They faced each other in front of a bank.

"I just came from your apartment. I went to visit you," he said.

She always knew what he would say. She smiled a lot and listened out of good humor. She threw little bunches of words at his face: drops of water on a hot day. He smiled without widening the glance-angle of his eyes. It stayed at her face.

"What are you doing today?"

She didn't need to answer such. More verbal tickling. "How I am a feather duster," she thought. "Maybe I am a French tickler." She used such expression without knowing its definition.

He bounced his eye now. It was a paddleball toy. His consciousness, if not his wooden head, got slapped by the bouncing. He believed in his resilience, though. "She will see the games this paddle can play. She will see how I can excel. I can stay under water longer than most without drowning."

Her attention was buttering down with heat from the 90 degree Fahrenheit sun. "Okay. You can take me for an hour. I don't resist," it said. She said, "I have calls to make. Illustrations to do. Can't see you now."

The acquaintance wanted more than these drops of water on his face, wanted more than a second's distraction from the sun. He wanted to tear with his nails the celluloid, the vestigial organs growing out of her back. He couldn't get close enough to cause even a scratch. He tapped a small, regular Indian pattern into the sidewalk with his toes. It washed into the other lines down there: graffiti, trails of cigarette wrappers, traces of smeared dog shit. There was a loud percussive sound. Her wings wanted to get on with it. She wiggled her shoulder blades, a pacifying action. The energy filtered into teeth gritting.

She skipped to her apartment. He skipped at a keeping up pace. She turned the phone dial, while he placed his rear haunches on her bed. "What are you doing?" she called into the room. (I see what you want, ducky.)

"I'm resting," he played back. (What else, oh strange lady?)

Presently and soon and before his effusive sweat could spread to the bed's blue blanket, she announced their leave-taking. "Outside awaits us." They took a rhythmic quick walk and arrived at a great cement Alphaville building.

"I don't want to go inside. Too nice out," she said.

It was his dormitory.

She took a different tack: "How my wrinkles are glistening." He did not get her small hint about the age difference between them. A reminder of equal men she was not meeting. She ran from the playpen after a polite pleading, a flirtatious refusal to accede to indoorness.

She sat on a park bench drawing as the wind blew hair patterns in front of her eyes. She drew through foreigners on the make, small boys on the edge of many questions, townies trying to get too close using their cameras as an excuse to try to touch her and to make vulgar jokes.

She left the park, an unholy leafless sandpit. She walked back to her apartment, single-framing facial features of too many sidewalk travelers. She took so many single frames, the appropriate index finger calloused, and her celluloid wings got dusty and bruised and in need of repair because of the wavering elbows of others. There would be no flight this night. She pasted the wings to a wall of her chamber. Many such wings (in disrepair) lined the wall. She grew new ones as her metabolism allowed.

Story.

A female had stopped walking. She was still
occupying a portion of the pavement. Her hands
were in an uncertain, temporary pose. If they could
have been chewing bubblegum, they would have.
Her face was pretty. A face like the young Leslie
Caron.

She had stopped there, by the parking meter, the
one with a coin slot that looked like a mouth. Her
long right thumbnail pointed to the metal stem of
the meter.

She was also in the company of a car. She was at
the mercy of steel. She was in the throes of metal
throbbing. Also, she had a headache. She yearned
for Dick Cavett or Donald Barthelme, a room and
some coffee. But she knew they were somewhere
else. Apart. And they were not yearning for her. She
had to get on with it. But she had frozen a few
circuits of her memory from hard travail, from
banging too hard with her head on metal, plastic,

glass and wood doors peopled by proprietors whose skins had taken on singularly inorganic sheens, they who would smile their almost accurate mimes of sympathy betraying only their own forever burned out circuitry.

She looked at the frog mascot that sat on the hood of the car. She had difficulty saying the word "frog" in her head. It kept coming out "FOG." She knew she should go to an island for a while. Bermuda, Jamaica, the Canary Islands, the British Isles. She could see the sand blowing into her eyes, though, and that was painful.

The next few days she stood in variations of the original pose, between other automobiles and parking meters on that street. Sometimes passersby took her for a fashion model. Mostly they didn't notice, though.

A dog drifted by and she liked its uniqueness and the way the dog had adjusted to such. A beagle-chihuahua. Following it for a few blocks, she forgot her variations on a stance and leaped into a tableau.

Three women stood against a wall, wearing flowered sunsuits of a bright yellow. They moved around as if a photographer induced them to with promises of rum sodas with apricot ice cream and guaranteed-to-attack guard dogs, a requisite item in this city. No photographer was in evidence, though. The female leaped again and noticed how much larger she was in mass than the sunsuit women. One of them stood on her shoulder saying, "What're you drawing?"

"What're you drawing?"

Female thought such was an amusing if not irrational thing to say, as she was not drawing at all. Nor could she. She was wondering if her car would get a parking ticket. She wanted to relieve her headache. The woman on her shoulder, she saw, was resting her hand on a second woman's head. This made the female's headache worse.

Some time later, a man walked into the room. He had a question mark affixed to his shirt, and spoke alternatingly in a meek, pleasant, understanding, wise voice and a confident, charming, selfish, inconsiderate one. All the women wished he had a third voice. But he didn't. He was there to sell them some Fuller Brushes.

"They're very useful for all sorts of things," he said, smiling and looking away shyly. A curl tumbled onto his collarbone. He shook the hair out of his face quickly. "They're good for cleaning toilets." He looked directly into the female's eyes for a full minute. She could not look away. He kept speaking. "For cleaning the family dog. For getting cobwebs out of ceiling corners." He puckered his lips. "I'm sure you'd be most happy to buy one." His eyes were smiling. He looked away. The female noticed his huge hands, his muscled arms.

She walked briskly and loudly out of the room, tossing her head in a goodbye gesture. She walked in such a manner for 15 or 20 blocks. Her cheeks were red. Her eyes were narrow and staring without blinking, sharp stares, as if she had two laser beams coming from inside her head. No trees burned in front of her. No dust particles showed any excess of motion. They didn't form any Busby Berkeley kaleidoscope patterns. No insects were tracked off their flights. She sat down, all the while praying to nothing she'd turn into a hedgehog. She did.

Chapter 18

Jombolaya heard her song on the radio a few weeks prior. But couldn't today or tomorrow, as:

1. Her radio had been stolen
2. She had no job, no money to buy a new one.

Jombolaya reminded herself of a small wooden toy you used to find in the 5 & 10 cent stores when there were such frivolities, or which were given out by itinerant suburban whip-men (who were found directing those horizontal ovoid rides kiddies occupy for a dime, called "The Whip" because at the edges of the ovals, the little carts would go especially fast around the tracks.)

The small toy consists of two strips of vertically parallel wood, between which is a toy monkey or man. When you squeeze the wooden handles together, the monkey or man dances a little frenzy-dance, which means he can use up all the energy being transmitted to him by the squeeze, but he can't go anywhere. Thus the curious toy contortions. But Jombolaya wasn't a toy.

She saw and heard all those injurious sights and sounds her environment provided. She had a small editing device, but it got clogged so often, and she cleaned it so infrequently, that mostly everything passed into her head, the flow-through teabag way. In, in, in, in, in, until she could take no more without having to also take soon-to-be-made comments by well meaning acquaintances: "swelled head!"

She took her head off and tried airing it out. But the impure air only added to the chazzerai.

Chapter 19

Orangia sprawls on a low bed. She effuses words, blended of anger and need of release. The climate is warm--no, hot--and humid. Orangia knows that the trees which are visible from two windows do not twist in the wind for her. She tries to get her focus off her skin, that heat-retaining substance. For many months now, Orangia sees only evenly spaced circles spew from her mouth each time she speaks. The circles are the same size as smoke rings, but opaque. They rise into parts of the upper atmosphere, not taking the time to invest in glory of being able to encircle common, on-the-ground objects, in the sense of strangulation. Orangia was dismayed in part at the inexplicable vanishment of her vocal cords, as well as at the cowardice of her small circles.

Chapter 20

semi-sentient

rapidly adaptable

Sally salamander sat, meandering in her head. She thought the same dullities again and again. "What's the use of reading book reviews?" thought Sally. "What's the good of writing?" She asked these and other questions of herself often. She really would've liked answers of another. But no ones she met ever had any answers; in fact, most of them hadn't even any questions. She was dismayed. She frayed. She was afraid.

Chapter 21

BACK TO TOTALITY. Qu'est ce qui s'ennui? -il faut écrire un roman si tu ne peux pas faire une filme. -ses ideés sont trôp important à attender pour l'argent pour faire une filme.

Chelsea Oregano found this note taped to the refrigerator as she walked into the kitchen of her apartment. The refrigerator door was already blackboard for the magazine photos of starving people she kept posted there. It kept her from complacency, even when she was hungry and her stomach said, "Security, a job with good pay! This is what we need!" Her stomach was a quiet, generally undemonstrative being. It spoke only out of great need.

Chelsea wondered out loud. Her voice bounced off the white walls. "Where the hell could this have come from?" She lived with no one. It was at this observation, the note on the refrigerator, that Chelsea allowed for the division of herself into the two modes or people of Chelsea Oregano and Jane Grain.

As the surface characteristics of the names would indicate, Chelsea was the frantic, frivolous one who invited chance, in the manner of youth. She sometimes bought a Chunky when she deserved good luck. She believed the two came together. Jane was heavier, with more gravity of personality. Jane was the one who packed quarters, nickels and dimes, tips from the waitress job, in their respective rolls. Chelsea took the pennies and placed them in tiny toy frying pans which she kept on windowsills in her bedroom. These served no noticeable function like the Chunkies, but provided a breathing space.

Chelsea wrote beautiful energy-packed paragraphs in monthly notebooks. None of the paragraphs connected. She sometimes mused on placing them together like dominoes. All the paragraphs with a protagonist named Sally would follow each other. But the Sally part was the only common denominator. Dominoes themselves were more consistent and orderly. Thus Chelsea knew it couldn't have been she who placed the well-advised note on the refrigerator door. It had to be someone else. And Jane Grain was born.

Here are some surface characteristics of the person herself, since you may be finding it hard to form a picture. She is in her mid-twenties. She doesn't like to lie. She doesn't like to ask someone how they are feeling when she doesn't give a damn. She can't feign interest in a heavy co-worker's chafing thighs, when she *has* no interest. So she stays away from people she isn't so crazy about, as much as possible. She sometimes wishes she hadn't such strong dislikes for lying. She would then be able to slide through all sorts of situations--especially job situations. Unfortunately (that is, coinciding with her basic incompatibility with lying), she has a grand ambition. She must make some far-reaching films, films that will yell loudly and universally as the 12 o'clock whistle does in all Amerikan towns, films that will be as freeing as changing society daily and instantly to suit all of our needs.

"She is dreaming," you say. "Pleasant dreams."

Oh, but they are not a bit pleasant, she would be the first one to tell you, anger in her eyes so that they are almost jumping out of her face and flying into yours. "They are painful dreams. I cannot *make* these movies."

Jane Grain interjects. "Napoleon once said 'Impossible is a word to be found only in the dictionaries of fools.' My dear soulmate, Chelsea, you are a fool."

Chelsea, smiling, answers in her usual charming manner. "Oh, but you wouldn't want me to be perfect now, would you? That would be a bore. Or if not, it would be an uncomfortable comparison for Other People, those who know me or don't. How stultifying to have to come into contact with a flawless person."

Why can't Chelsea make these movies? Why are shoe repairmen so often Italian immigrants? Why do writers invariably turn into drunks? Why doesn't some actress make a fervent a plea for women as Marlon Brando did, rejecting his Oscar in protest, for American Indians?

Chelsea's constant trying to rise in the film hierarchy had made her into a trying person. She was trying especially on her own patience, nerves.

She walked from her apartment to a bus. On the way she passed a corner house that was being painted shiny gray-blue. Lots of young guys were the painters. They hardly ever looked down from their ladders in curiosity. Chelsea felt today like a cockroach coming out of a kitchen crack, walking past these paint guys yet again. She was the town's only pedestrian. And even that might be changed with the results of the bicycle lottery.

She was drifting. Wingless drifting--that is, not drifting to see the clouds and feel the air. Drifting of exhaustion from being a tireless job seeker. Her throat had become lately raspy, a reaction to the yelling. Each time she presented herself for a job, she'd stand there, red cheeked and smiling, in her high school cheerleader uniform, and go through a sufficiently tantalizing repertoire. "Rah! Rah! Sis-Boom-Bah! Hi-re Me and You'll Go Fah!" "C*H*E*L*S*E*A. I'm The One To Hire ToDay!" The bosses in charge of hiring would sit at curious attention, interrupting their steady stare only occasionally to take a phone call. When they addressed her, as was necessary at the completion of her presentation, they did so in a hedging, faltering, downright nervous voice. "Miss, Miss, uh..." They'd cough and look unsubtly down at the resume.

They'd hire her then, on the spot. She'd maintain her composure under the heading "Miss All American Girl" for a while. For as long, in fact, as she could veritably stand the pose.

But in not too long a time, it would come leaking--or worse, leaping--out, bit by honest bit.

"I'm glad Marlon Brando did that. There should be more--scores and millions--and more people like him," she would say to the bossman, her enthusiasm for Good Actions needing to show itself.

The boss would remove the cigarette or cigar from his hand, allowing the poisonous smoke to suffuse the air around Chelsea's face, especially her sensitive, contact-lens-covered eyes, and beg to differ. Not that he would beg. Mostly he would differ. Chelsea made every attempt to check her own opinions right there. To create yes-nods of her head, affecting tacit agreement with said bossman. But her honesty would not be suppressed.

And Chelsea would find herself dismissed from that employ by the next morning.

****

1. She rolled across a field. Some children had grown up in this farmhouse, having nothing impinging on their view of the sky for all those years. Having nothing in the way to create shadows

around the house. Chelsea rolled, over and over, left side to right, left side, right side. Ironing the grass. Staining her dungarees. Smelling the fresh ground, dandelions and daisies and peppermint.

2. Chelsea was in a library, thinking. "There are some topics I must learn to their depths, immediately." One was economics. One was physics.

3. She got home with an armload of books and found another refrigerator note:

TYING, TYING. TYING THE ENDS
TOGETHER. THE MEANS AND THE
ENDS. ALL OF THE MANY OF THEM.
ROLLING THEM INTO A UNIFIED
WOOL BALL. KNITTING SOMETHING
FINER THAN A SWEATER FROM IT.

4. Chelsea waited on a sunny street for a bus. She wore sunglasses. She was a female. She darted behind a telephone pole to hide, like so many slick, crafty foxes do in so many cartoons.

Jane is standing, hands on hips. Belligerent, like.
"Chelsea, you are entirely rebellious, in the context
within which you keep yourself, here among the
faithful early rise work people. They don't have
crayons on the shelves in their bedrooms. They
have flour on the shelves in their kitchens. Most
people (of this realm) can be located easily. Just
ring up the number of their work company and there
they are, on the far side of the phone cable. Hello,
Shirley. Hello, Bill. Hello, Peggy. But Chelsea, how
is one to locate you, if one would?"

Chelsea: "Those that would are able. Have it within
their reach, my location. My whereabouts. Those
that ought, don't, though. I know not why." Chelsea
is reading a paper called "BUMS." She has several
marbles in her mouth.

Shirley says, "Chelsea!! How _are_ you? Guess
what!! I'm getting married!!"

Bill says, "How're ya doin'?"

Peggy says, "Oh! What're you doing now?"

Chelsea spits out the answers (but not the marbles). The truth, tired as it is. An exaggeration. An avoidance. A petty lie.

1. Don't ask!! (The truth, tired as it is.)
2. I am hanging from a trapeze by my elbows. It is for a Jergen's dry skin cream commercial.
3. I am sleeping.
4. I am not. Naught.

Chelsea phoned all these bookkeepers in search of her missing W-2 tax forms. All three companies fired her, in Cambridge and Boston. One of the companies is a temporary-job agency. She'd been dismissed from the credit card office of a bank. She'd been proofreading sums of numbers and to alleviate some of the boredom, proofread some of the permanent employees, who in their boredom spoke and smiled to her. Talking and smiling are not permitted concurrently in temporary employees. This was a rule Chelsea had difficulty aligning herself with.

According to a *New York Times* article, Columba University researchers found in a "Tolerance for Bureaucratic Structures" test that those people easiest to remold in a job training program are older, female, married, black and Protestant. Those most resistant to remolding are young, single, highly or poorly educated, Puerto Rican or white, and Jewish or Catholic.

From this information, Chelsea could rewrite her occasional wish for assimilation into society in more detail. Instead of just wishing NOT to be an artist, a critic, she could wish to be a middle-aged married Protestant woman. Margaret Earp. (Great granddaughter of Wyatt Earp.) Second cousin on her mother's side to Davy Crockett III. Dirty blonde hair turned gray and left that way. Colonial furniture all through the house. Baked ham on the table. A Ford in the driveway. *Reader's Digest* in the mailbox. Hometown: Biloxi. Tea with honey. An occasional dry martini with a twist. Husband in the basement. Barbecue in the backyard. Never heard of lox or Norman Mailer. Children: Maggie, braless at 15. Tom, an R.O.T.C. man. Tim, an engineering student at West Point. Maggie taken to unreported excursions with Red, the family's Irish setter, who she has renamed Laudatory.

Margaret to her husband, Jim: "Where is Maggie?"

Jim, from the cellar: "Beats me."

"Where is Red?"

Jim: "Dunno." He shugs his shoulders in front of the ping pong table, where Tom waits for a serve, Schlitz in hand, Marlboro in ashtray, smoke dimming the air.

Maggie on haunches in the forest. Laudatory hunting for snakes. Maggie has been reading witchcraft manuals and is stocking up. She slides the found snakes into an old stocking, rewarding Laudatory with a biscuit. The air is moist and fogged. No sun. Branches crackle underfoot.

Tom and Tim have formed a partnership. They have

an engineering consulting firm. Maggie thinks engineering is the dullest of all. Tom, who smokes a pipe, is in charge of hiring. He inserts a Secretary Wanted ad in the local paper. Ten people call the next day. One of them is a young man. "Sorry," Tom says to him over the phone, "That position is already filled." Five women come for interviews the next morning. Four in the afternoon. The third one is stacked and has long auburn hair. She can only type 20 words a minute. He hires her at the end of the day.

****

Chelsea is still reading *BUMS*, the only newspaper she subscribes to. It is filled with stories, much like any newspaper, but they are of bums.

Adam Blakely, 27, of Biggstown, Iowa, collects unemployment. Voted "most likely to succeed" in his high school yearbook, he was an English major at Antioch. He is reading all English novels published between 1910-1911 this month. For relaxation, he screams "Let there be light" twice daily, while he is ringing the bells of the town cathedral. He receives $5 a day for this. Curiously, although he bears no resemblance, his friends call him Quasimodo. They are construction workers and have long blonde hair and fabulous arm muscles. They all have girlfriends who they are living with. Adam does not, because he is so choosy. He likes Tracy Nelson and Shulamith Firestone and Bianca Jagger and Anna Karina a lot. He doesn't find any girls in his daily life who are scintillating in any way.

Adam looks like Joe D'Allesandro's double. He got his arm muscles from ringing the cathedral bells. He never yawns anymore, as he used to when he was an elevator operator. He left all his yawns there, in the elevator, on the day he was fired. That was the day he hung a photo of Richard Nixon defecating, on the back wall of the elevator. Nobody seemed to mind the pictures of bowls of Campbell's tomato soup, or Ivory soap or Doeskin tissues, but this one of Nixon on the toilet inexplicably took them aback. Adam sat there, opening and closing the door, monitoring the sound levels of the hidden microphone, as they went from floor to floor to floor.

Chelsea loves this newspaper. She sends a gift subscription to Kevin Ayers, an English singer-songwriter, for being so doughty and stubborn in the face of it all. Then she takes a nap while Jane cooks dinner.

Chapter 22

Chelsea was standing in the middle of the living room and kicking up her heels, one at a time. First slowly, with a minute between the alternating kicks. Then faster and faster.

"What are you doing, Chelsea?" Jane asked, in her annoying manner instead of using her admittedly deflated imagination.

"I'm practicing courage in the face of adversity," answered Chelsea.

"Adversity?"

"Yes, the adversity of un- or under-employment. And by the way, Jane Grain, you remind me of a wedgie. You like the practicality of being a flat, yet you prefer the raised style consciousness of being high as a heel. Jane Grain, you have nothing to worry about. You will never go insane. You are a wedgie. You are oozing with symptoms of Brain Drain. You, in being this wedgie, escape the epithets of Plain Jane, and, to a lesser extent, Vain Jane."

Jane was seething. Small round drops of mercury gathered around her feet, in a "the wicked witch is melting" image. Chelsea didn't notice, in her calculated rage of destruction. Jane melted slowly, not as the wizard of Oz's wicked witch at all. A few more mercury drops gathered around her feet. Then, in a fluttering of light, and one still photo image of her overlapping another...flash! flash! flash! Jane was making her angry way back into the psyche of Chelsea. Committee for a Unified Chelsea. Chelsea didn't get dizzy or have a sneeze attack. She didn't get tired suddenly or gradually as if her lungs had been invaded by Carbon Monoxide. She didn't enter a paroxysm of creativity, singing new and enchanting lyrics without a thought or moment's notice. She didn't acquire a renewed ability to convert all matter and circumstance into mathematical equations. She had no urges to run to the playground swings and rip them down, one by one, chain or not. No. She continued her soliloquy, alluding to William Gass and Anne Wiazemsky and summoning the departed spirits of Harpo Marx and Rilke to that very spot. Harpo, in his spirit world (actually, Jupiter), was indulging in a bowl of canned beans. They had just been taken out of the can and warmed. Rilke, in his world, either Venus or the North Star, was blowing a small flying insect off a sheet of typing paper. Venus or the North Star had recently been invaded by a world of these small insects. They did nothing but crawl on sheets of typing paper, which they were strangely attracted to.

Chapter 23

How Chelsea is different, now that Jane Grain has
joined her.

1. She is thinner. This isn't so logical, because, if
   you remember, Jane Grain was heavy. Like, oh,
   200 pounds, roughly. And she stood 5'5" without
   shoes. Chelsea isn't *so* much thinner than she
   was before, now that Jane Grain has joined her,
   only five pounds. And she still looks fine.

2. She returns to an invention she'd begun a year
   ago. It is a game for children, adults and those who
   don't care which they are. Mostly, it is for this last
   category. They are the ones who are most
   concerned with understanding this particular
   society. The game has a name: Priorities. Chelsea
   has invented two thirds of it. What it needs, mostly,
   now, is polish and arm muscle. She has the polish.

The arm muscle she has to find. She sets out to.
Not, you must understand, that the game requires
physical strength to be completed. No, not physical
strength in-itself, but rather physical strength once-
removed, as concerns the completion of the
remaining third. Chelsea is missing a boyfriend.
Particularly one with large arms and muscles
thereof. A particular boyfriend. Not, in this case,
one in the abstract. Chelsea, despite all her exercises
to the contrary, in the rational, disciplined chambers
of her conscious mind, cannot forget this one. In
fact, due to memories of him, the only thing she can
look at with desire, in her everyday life, is a
squirrel.

Chapter 24

Chelsea awoke from a daydream at 10 to 4 in the morning because she heard a coyote. Her daydream was as impossible, it seemed to her, as the coyote: who ever heard of a coyote in Princeton, NJ, the only town that could go for McGovern in the Presidential election and look like it still lived in the 1940s or at least in the throes of the Clean-for-Gene campaign? There was not a dynamic artist-longhair in town. These here town folk were all very deliberate in their actions; to tie a shoelace was a matter of correct time and place, to be sure.

Oh, a coyote. Such a nice surprise in this cultural aridity! These town folk manufactured culture. Stale. Stale before it was even conceived, because the people ate breakfast lunch and dinner breakfast lunch and dinner breakfast lunch and dinner backwards. That was their one structural talent: they could bend their knees and bodies backwards. But, unfortunately, they used their talents for all the wrong things.

Chelsea opened the front door to invite the coyote in for some milk. She wasn't sure if coyotes preferred milk. But alas, the creature was nowhere to be seen. Chelsea cried.

Chapter 25

She stood, short in height, shorter in breath--
breathless, maybe--across the street from a three-
story building. Both she and the building were
under a coat of rain. They did not huddle for
warmth. She cringed, dazed and humble, gazing at a
second story window, its fogged surface, and
beyond that to a desk lamp lit, and the wall of books
beyond. She saw no face. No magnetic hand
reached out the window to draw her tin soul nearer.
She was very near already, if not her plastic body,
then at least her now-wet, tin soul. Danger of rust?
No. She'd been rust-proofed as a child, when her
affliction--rather her curious mutation--was
discovered. How <u>was</u> it discovered? She was
intensely attracted to magnetic thinkers, such as
Jeffrey Townsend, Archimedes Blake, David R.S.
Full.

She left her idler's position. She left her idol's

window.

Later she awoke. It was Sunday afternoon, raining. She was home, in an over-soft mattress, which kept her in its middle.

She was all alone. She begged him whose window she watched last night, "Please don't let your eyes turn to diamonds." But she was too late in her thinking, too late in her observation; in the wrong style in her supplication.

1. His eyes were already diamonds. Not, anymore, diamond-like.
2. He resisted women who sought his returned interest through supplication and entreatment. He preferred the ones with rippling backs and kicking legs. Kicking in offense.

Chelsea set to work on yet another novel. This one was called "aggressing."

Chapter 26

Wilhelmina Glitter sat amuck amid her blue blanket folds. "Humanity, fah," she said with a toss of her head. This was a new gesture in her nonverbal vocabulary. She entered another room.

She turned on a water faucet, to wash her face. No water came out, only loud screeching sounds.

She had faltered. Once a star, she had followed her Ambition from one cockroach-ridden apartment to another faulty-peopled apartment.

Then she lost it, as its rope was loosening her natural set of teeth. She preferred real teeth to ambition.

"Hello, hello, hello," she sang to the empty mailbox attached to the porch wall. The mailbox remained silent.

Wilhelmina ate the dust for breakfast, with milk and sugar. She never was drunk. She only felt drunk. Lightheaded, uncommitted to anything but her cobwebby dreams.

She had fever often. She wrapped her head in old newspapers. They only made her more aware of the accomplishment-proud others.

She wrote songs about pepper. She swallowed a lot, feeling the red of her throat.

She dreamt of cows and lambs, <u>not</u> steak and lamb chops.

Her housemates' spare time activities breathed of congealment: baking, sewing.

She knew nothing of the sticky substance of egg, that which held the cake's dry ingredients together; she knew nothing of the connecting ability of thread, that which held together cloth and cloth.

Chapter 27

She lived in a room among scraps of paper and
walls of framed nouns. All her verbs died, as did the
plants, not getting enough sun or getting too much
water.

She was tired of verbs. She spat at any that flew in
the window now.

She was warped from all the water left over from
the drenched, dead plants, memories unerasable as
the warp she saw every time she faced a mirror.

I am Quasimodo, she smiled malevolently. She
couldn't really help it.

Chapter 28

On the refrigerator door, Chelsea posted a song she had composed. It went to the tune of "You are my Sunshine."

You are my cynosure,
My only cynosure
You make me happy
When skies do frown,
You'll never know, probably
How much I have you
Please don't break my cynosure down.

She hummed it on the way to half a grapefruit or a piece of celery. She hummed it in her hunger and when the cupboard was bare. She hummed it while washing dishes and when she turned the warm water on, only to have the water come out full blast boiling, onto the sponge, onto her hand. She hummed it in the hall and in the bedroom. She sang it in her head while bleating past the furry neighbors tending their paltry and bland flocks. Hi, she waved, more to the sheep than to the shepherds, on her way to the supermarket for some crumbs.

"Will it be breadcrumbs or graham cracker crumbs?" asked the pimply soap stocker. He was the one who made sure his soap stock was flush level before he turned his head to the questioning customer. Bureaucratic little spigot.

Chapter 29

Sally had many key words, from time to time. Once, an art student, her key word was Focus. She made a small viewing device from a rectangle of paper. A few years later, no longer a student, the word was Priorities. She invented a children's board game of the same name. It grew so complex, it became an adult's board game. Sally abandoned it. The complexity caused her to abandon key words, in fact. Now she had no key word at all. If she were forced to coin one, it would be "breathe."

She was back to her old game of spite. Spiting time. Or, rather, spiting that society which pressed the concept of time into her so fully, so well, that she dismayed at not using it to her utmost. While dismaying, she made invisible lists of the possible ways of using that time. And of the ensuing percentage of benefit. She used more time weighing the possibilities, indeed, than in actualizing any of

them. Stasis. She would spite time by <u>not</u> using it.
She sat on time, pressing all the air out of its lungs.
She would sit for hours doing nothing. Gazing at a
patch of air, gloating over her wastefulness. How
extravagant I am. I have not money to throw to the
winds in expressions of my hatred for this society. I
must waste what I have. But she didn't smile much
while so occupied. And the walls, alas, did not
smile back at her.

Chapter 30

After doing somersaults on variations on the theme
of job categories: salaries, satisfaction in a job,
Sally started noticing the simple yet elegant words
against the air. The ones that floated around every
day, but weren't noticed, not due to arrogance or
neglect or disbelief, but merely due to lack of time
to look at the air. After all, briefcase
hauling/dragging (sometimes, even, as with a
stubborn dog, tugging) took at least all one's
viewing energy.

You're wondering, even wishing you could ask the
writer, was Sally a bit schizoid, that is, even
schizophenic? She looked at the air. That was her
eccentricity. Oh, several times, she mistook her own
hair for a cockroach, but otherwise--naw.

Do you pull your window shades down at night? Do
you live on a very narrow street, so narrow that cars
are only allowed to park on one side, and do you
face a school administration building with loads of

windows whose inhabitants arrive on their jobs very early in the morning?

Do you have geraniums on the floor that require lots and lots of light? And do you then wake up very early to lift the shade covering the ceiling-to-floor window so as not to deprive them of any?

Do none of these questions apply to you, oh reader? Then I suggest you turn to page 82 of the paperback version of Donald Barthelme's *Snow White*.

Chapter 31

Story

Drawing stood on one side, smiling confidently. Writing stood on the other, smiling, but we knew it was a smile of fear. Writing smiled to cover its lack of ease, but we saw the worry in its eyes. We, the audience, had assembled to vote. Some were merely onlookers, nonpartisan curiosity seekers. Some felt staunch and self-righteous as Joseph McCarthy in a jury for ANY BEATNIK. I watched the audience as well as the opponents, who stood in their corners getting rubdowns. Perry Mason and Sherlock Holmes were prominent front row sitters. We all waited for the bell. Samuel Beckett and Mick Jagger had been invited, but, of course, neither attended or returned their negative response cards.

Drawing took a step forward. "What the hell is this?" it said, forthrightly, "a chess game?" Every time I make a move," it puts its hands on its hips, "You, Writing, mimic me."

Writing put hands on hips (unintentionally mimicking Drawing) in an assertive gesture. "I'd call it competition, in the best American spirit..."

"Ho," said Drawing, scornfully. "What do you know of spirit, you who require stories and stand on your head with technique shining around you like a spotlight at the grand opening of a Korvettes store."

"Ah," said Writing. "Now who's mimicking whom? How dare you use verbal imagery in your offense. How dare you!"

At this point in the debate, Music wafted in, slowly but steadily, stealing the attention of the audience and certainly distracting the debaters.

Fortunately for the weaker one, the bell rang, summoning both back to their corners for a damp towel and a glass of ice water each.

The audience buzzed opinions, overcoming the music, even. Music had attention needs of its own, or shall we say, needs to use its heady talents, which were packing into its head double-, triple-parking style, so that poor Music, who was getting a migraine, sang louder.

The audience, busy debating among themselves, didn't register the increasing volume. They only were conscious of something annoying, like the undefined loud sound of an air conditioner. Relief when it stops, but unconsciousness of its fogging the mind waves.

Drawing and Writing simultaneously reached out towards omnipresent Music, to swat it like a fly. But Music being as big as it is in any given space, they could at best only pinch a tiny part of it. Like a pin prick, or a mosquito bite that doesn't get red or swell or itch. Drawing and Writing became very frustrated. Not only was their debate up to this round a stalemate, but they could not deter this pretender to the throne. What nerve Music had, they each thought in their respective modes.

Their frustration turned into loud yelling, crying,

screaming, so that they each usurped a large part of Music's air waves. So large a part, that Music's large volume was getting squashed, pushed into itself. Music began emitting curses of static and lower volume. Soon, Music was so pushed into itself, it couldn't be heard anymore.

Drawing and Writing, realizing what they had done together, walked each towards the other and shook hands. They would have embraced, but in the year of this debate, sentiment was scorned upon, was not the fashion.

Chapter 32

Olivia walked on a windy street, reaching out, recklessly, for blowing "moneystealers," those seedpods mythically connected with having one's wish. She reached to get the seedpod, and her arm almost separated from the rest of her, but the pod managed to exceed her grasp.

"Anyone who is not handicapped," said the radio, "has a hard time imagining what it's like to be handicapped. There are problems. Small ones, like..." Olivia was about to turn off the radio, but left it on when it said, "Big ones, like not being able to find an apartment or a job."

"Well then, I may as well be handicapped," she thought.

****

"I believe in synthesis," Sally said.

"I believe in synthetic," Richard Nixon's mother said when he was a little boy.

"I believe in God," said a priest.

"I believe in shovellin' shit," said Steppin Fetchit and a chorus of *Playboy* bunnies.

"I don't believe in anyone but me, Yoko and me," said John Lennon.

From idealism to pragmatism. From change to playing with mud while Oz burns. Art. What is art but sophisticated distraction? How can we rationalize it? Why must we? It keeps coming through our questions of "Should we feel overly sensitive to feel guilty for playing so?" Or is this play our only safety valve against individual (as opposed to societal) brain damage?

"Whaddya mean, synthesis?" demanded Groucho, cigar hanging out of mouth, while Harpo demonstrated. "There will be no separation of the activity one does to earn one's keep from what one does the rest of one's time."

Chapter 33

ON THURSDAY,
Maisie Crazy Daisy Lazy goes to Boston's Logan
Airport for a job. Seeing the wide spaces of visible
sky makes her smile. She is feeling dishonest to be
going to the airport without intending to board a
plane, as if she ought to tell everyone she
encounters (starting with the bus driver) that she is
really only at the airport to find a job. Her feet are
hurting from the stupidity she has done: bought a
pair of uncomfortable shoes for their beauty. She
pulls both ends of the rope around her neck, but this
doesn't move her forward; it gives her chafe marks.
She resents being admired for physical attributes,
yet feels miscast to be less than well attired. She
manages to be given two job applications for
domestic airlines. If she'd felt just a little gloomier,
she would have applied to be an airline stewardess.

Oh, but all these jobs are unsatisfying. Wasn't there
ANY situation, ANYWHERE that would enable her
to work somewhere near her potential? It wasn't

even a case of being spoiled. It was a case of grand insecurity: the need to prove oneself, to be recognized for one's abilities. She admired, and wished she could trade (places) with, anyone who had a job they could stick with because they liked it. The only job she'd ever had that she looked forward to attending every morning was one in an art supply store. It was a very ordinary and boring job, but she loved looking at a sexy co-worker. He always looked back at her but was married.

She wanted to throw rocks at her sensitivity, that which made her into a hermit at times like these. She wanted to have naturally red cheeks and be brave and bold and say anything she liked to anyone she encountered. But she was slip sliding into the bad, bathetic days of junior high school.

She had had it with the harsh vendors of you know not what. She still could wiggle her toes. She WAS breathing. Every now and then, sounds would make their way to her ears. Sounds of others--their transportation, their footsteps, their coughs, their laughs.

****

She was melting into the grass. Only her nose was now visible, the bump and the tip of it. A squirrel danced over so she could lick its chest. The squirrel was sometimes blue, sometimes gray.

It said to her, "Hey you, why aren't you gathering nuts for the winter?" At this point, by some odd coincidence of fantasy, they both heard in the air (They thought it was the air, but it really was in their heads) Helen Merrill singing "The Winter of Our Discontent."

She answered the squirrel. "Hey, man, I think you're nuts. Imagine a squirrel <u>talking</u>! Squirrels can't talk!"

The squirrel, hurt by this slur on his self, removed his tail, dusting it from side to side of her face.

"We may be in London, we may be in Boston. There is no difference, anyway."

"Indeed," Maisie muttered, mostly placatingly.

The squirrel, a male or a neuter, lay down on his back to take a sunbath.

Maisie was stifled. She'd tried that, and the ground turned to quicksand, leaving only parts of her nose above ground.

The squirrel, a while later, brought Maisie Gogol's book The Nose, which neither of them had read. He'd borrowed it from the Boston Public Library. Rumor had it that the squirrel was really a person with a spell on him (or it). This has been an advert for your public library. Hope you could relate to it.

Chapter 34

Sally was of average build. That is to say, she did
not have any bulging muscles, was not overly
strong at physical tasks. Added to this was the fact
that she'd never learned to swim properly. She had
been a bit of a know-it-all child. Not overly
appreciative of "The Way" to do anything, as
standard ways go, she preferred to stay above water
(which is how she regarded swimming) "her own
way."

Years later, she excused her lack of proper method
by mentioning her contact lenses. It would not do to
have them fall out while she was ducking her face
with each swim stroke. Thus she was not having a
fun time of it out [t]here in the deeps, off the coast
of New Jersey. How did she get [t]here? Oh, in the
logical, chronological way. Not that she didn't ask
herself that very question once every other thought.
She had plenty of time to think; the boat had
capsized only three hours ago, and she'd been doing

nothing but thinking and struggling to stay above water without fatiguing. She was managing, if not well, adequately. Her contact lenses hadn't fallen out; they were only a little bit fogged, thanks to the sun, which appeared from behind the clouds as regularly as her thoughts of "What am I doing here?"

She'd been on the boat, a ferry between New Jersey and work, eating potato chips and watching some children think they were dogs. They were talking, giggling dogs who barked only when they were at the feet of an adult. She was thinking the only way the adults might play along would be if they were drunk. She was wishing she could play along with the dog-children, but was all too conscious of the rest of the adults on the ferry. She smiled at one of the kids and, next thing she knew, the boat lurched, the loud speaker's "On" sound appeared--but static sounding, with no message--and people started losing their footing. No one knew what was wrong. She heard patches of speech. "...tidal wave...engine gone crazy...gravity amiss..." Then the water was all around her. Up to her hips, up to her chin. The ferry was sinking. Some people clung to it, others swam for shore.

She was in no hurry at first, preferring to enjoy the water and the excuse to stay out of work. It was a beautiful and hot day. She floated on her back for a while, and when she next looked around, no one was in sight. Land was barely visible and she knew she hadn't the stamina to swim all those miles. She was hungry and her mind was closing around a large, empty space. She swam towards land quickly, stopping when her breath was going faster than her arms. Land was still incredibly far away.

She started cursing herself, at first just a little bit. "Oh Sally, you've gone and done it now. You and your love of nature. Everyone else was practical and acted within reason, swimming back to shore. But you, Sally, had to stay out here and take a swim. You, who never even swim at the Y, who never even go to the beach more than twice a summer."

As her swims toward shore grew shorter and more numerous, her chides at self grew louder and angrier. "Sally, you fucking idiot." She stopped yelling to conserve energy.

She looked at her hands and saw little wormlike wrinkles on her fingertips. The water was not so dirty that it smelled bad or bore bits of scabrous material. It was almost clear, like chicken broth, an unlikely state for New Jersey coastal waters. She peered through it hoping to see alphabet noodles. She knew this was just her ordinary imagination, and she hadn't gone into the void of sunstroke yet. She feared a chill soon. She was biting her salty lip. There were goose pimples on her arms. She was getting bored, and wished there were someone out here to talk to. She sang, "Water, water everywhere, Everywhere, Everywhere, water, water everywhere, and I'm not even thirsty. Oh for some french fries. Oh for some water moccasins, oh for a water pipe, oh, oh, oh. Water, water everywhere and I can't swim."

Sally remembered the movie "Exterminating Angel" by Bunuel. She couldn't say she loved it. It was at best all right. And mostly boring. This was due to the unbelievability of it. Imagine a bunch of people who couldn't manage to leave the party they were at, who stayed there for weeks because some strange force kept them from wanting to leave, from leaving. She intensely hated creators who thought their audiences would accept such amazingly contrived story lines. But then it occurred to her that this hatred was related to her own dallying with the Contrived. She hated it, but couldn't avoid its charm and glitter.

Cows enthralled her now. She visited one in the zoo. "Sally," it said to her in a matter-of-fact, grainy and low voice, "You've gotta stop chewing your own cud. Take it from me. I'm a cow. I have to face it. I've been chewing my own cud for years now, and where does it get me? Some gray-tempoed, nondescript man sits beside me and handles, squeezes my lowers every day. He takes what comes out and I must take what comes. What do I get? Only *tsuris*." (It was a Jewish cow named Yetta.) "You've gotta find a new wrinkle. Sprout wings and find a new land or something. But stop chewing. Cavities, canker sores, pursed lips, whaddya need 'em for? Believe me, Sally, find a new. Find a New."

Sally thanked her for the advice, so well-timed, and set out for a New. It wouldn't be via water. The return to shore had been too unduly strenuous and tepid an activity for her. She considered scoring the outer page ends of a college dictionary and opening it where her fingernail stopped. Then she would scan the page with her fingertip, eyes closed. And the resulting word would be a clue to the New that Yetta held forth. But such whimsy had left her when she left London, three years ago. She could not be a dog-child any more than those other ferryboard adults could. She opened her eyes wide and breathed out. An expression of anger.

What did contrived mean to her? It meant Power over the randomness of chance. Chance dictated who one met and when and where and how long one had to wait to meet compatible people, people who one could admire. Fate also determined one's occupation, the occupation of one's days, whether one would be allowed to make a living the way one

was best able. Sally sought to contrive those ends.
She could not respect fate's decisions much,
anymore. Fate didn't know what was best for her.
Maybe it did for some, but she was not one of those.

Sally consulted the dictionary. Here was one she
respected. It did what it set out to do. It was concise
and accurate. No loose edges. It worked, the way
equations do. *Contrived*: "Adj. Obviously planned
or forced; artificial." That was what she hated about
the concept of Contrived: it was artificial. One butts
one's hard head against a brick wall and instead of a
softness forming in the wall, a softness forms in the
head; this was the misfortune of Contrived. How
much more appropriate to have an easy smile. More
appropriate than a determined grin. "Easy" was
such a smooth word. It smelled of clover and raw
spinach. "Determined" smelled of rectangularity
and metal bolts. Sally had become so metallic, she
didn't emit a smell at all. Just a painfully blinding
shine. The kind of shine one doesn't prefer, as in
ironing-a-pair-of-trousers shine.

She reminded herself of the tin man from the

Wizard of Oz. Water fell on her and she knew she'd be rusting soon. Sally looked around, dazed. She was IN the water. Oh, no!

She was still in the water off the coast of New Jersey. The elements had made her doze off for a while, into that state between sleep and wakefulness. "Shit!" she reacted to her stay in the deeps. "I should have a bunch of postcards," she thought, "saying 'Having a great time. As yet have seen no mermen or -maids, not even a sea cow resembling Yetta, but otherwise, the weather is fine, the food is exotic.'

"What IS the food?" thought Sally. "I'm starving! That's what's causing these peculiar thought arrangements to enter my mind."

She spit half a mouthful of water back into the Atlantic. The drizzle was subsiding, but she was still very cold. Land was pretty close now. Only two or three of her short, fast swims and she'd be on sand. "I bet my lips are very blue." She looked into the water to see, but it wasn't reflecting colors. "Funny, there have been no sharks or electric eels or swordfish or jellyfish to scare me." There was the Goodyear blimp overhead. It was late afternoon. "They must wonder where I am, at work. I've only been working there two weeks." Sally worked in a doughnut factory. She sprinkled sugar on cruellers. She'd rather her pay-the-rent job be something like putting the holes in the doughnuts, so at least it would be metaphysical fun instead of the complete bore it was. She was thinking about holes in doughnuts as she darted a fast swim towards the ever-nearing shore. "I feel like an old movie serial. In episode 98, the log the heroine is tied to rolls within two inches of the electric saw. In episode 99, she and her log have made backward progress, and the state of immanent danger has been lengthened in time. Here I swim once more. Am I moving backwards, indeed?"

What Sally could not know, she was swimming on that old iceberg of parable fame. The more she swam towards shore, with all her effort and all her good humor, the more the iceberg beneath the water drifted further out to sea. Some would call it a stalemate. Some would say treadmill. Sally would have called it unjust. She was young enough yet to be making such distinctions.

Chapter 35

She was pouring sweet cream and small flowers

into her friend's mailbox. Her plans backfired:

The bees got there before he did. Her friend

connected the mailbox of bees to her signature.

"This woman has hostility," he declared. He se-

cured an exterminator to rid his mailbox of its

tenants. And went back to a breakfast of tea

and toast-with-jam.

On being told that one has insidious hostility by a
perceptive stranger one has met 2 years later

Chapter 36

Shelby tripped along the Harvard bridge, squinting. He hopped occasionally, half-smiling at passing cars. His left foot was dangling from his left calf; it wasn't so happy about the hopping, being left to spill through the air, through space, without donating a bit of weight to gravity, the American way.

Shelby, comprised of a lot more than left and right feet, was feeling spunky. The discontent of the lower member hadn't yet sung its way, screaming, to the rest of him, so he continued his spurt-sprint across the bridge. From time to time, he spat into the waters. Not in indignation, not in affectation; he spat to give his spit a chance to swim.

Some sliding sorceress saw Shelby spit. She giggled, much out of character for a witch, not to disguise her position (as she was not so self-conscious as other witches) but only because she thought it extremely funny that a spirited stranger should be spitting on such a sunny February day.

Shelby didn't catch her tremor or her eye, but concentrated on hubcaps. He hoped to see some loose ones as he hopped his last quarter of the bridge.

Chapter 37

This morning I awoke from too short a sleep; someone was trying to telegraph a message to me. The tapping was clear and loud and consistent. But I have no receiver. I was upset. Not because I have no receiver; I noticed I was being derivative. I hate being derivative. I hate being derivative and too tired to sleep. Also I was being repetitive, though it was too early to know whether such was intentional or a natural, even likely outgrowth of my sleep-deprived state.

My eyes asked to be elsewhere. They cried, they burned. I tried to comply. But I kept being distracted by the birds near my room. They were in a mood to entertain. They don't, can't know about such states as mine.

I turned the light switch on the lamp. I turned my body in the bed. I hoped to spiral into sleeplessness. The electric blanket made a croaking sound. It was more on the side of the birds than on the side of me.

I punished it for such noises by pushing much of it beneath me. Its thermostat doesn't like such insubordination from a mere non-object. I waited for further croaks. Protest. I didn't have to wait for long.

The morning rain had stopped. The soothe of its sound was replaced by an angry blanket, croaking.

I tried to sleep again. It defied me.

I sighed.

****

Today is the second week of March and 70 degrees
and sunny. I walk from McCarter Theatre, across
Nassau Street and down Madison to my house and
find the streets littered with swarms of bearded men
who appear out of nowhere, like worms in the rain.

I like to go over each of D.B.'s sentences slowly,
savoring them, the way one sucks a chocolate
covered carmel instead of chewing it. But I am too
hungry and must go quickly.

****

She felt as if every strand of her perceptive fiber
was out seeking its own end. She, the sum, though,
had to be moving from one room to the other, from
one group of people to another, and on to others.
She had to ignore the pulling and tugging of her
attention centers.

And thus, she felt crazy. She put the spoon in the Russian dressing and the latter jumped up to hit her face in little splotches. She got a dishrag and removed those. She returned to the Russian dressing; it happened again.

She wanted to catch the fragments of overheard conversations and put them in her apron pocket with the tips. Money and words. Oil and water. The world and her.

She was able to practice humility at times, mostly as a defense or a deceit. As experience had slapped it to her, she knew that her actual, natural speaking self was not appreciated by bosses, proprietors of those companies she plodded a half-living from; by those who acted but did not really feel like her superiors. (What was sad was that they had the need to feel as such.)

And so she pushed her real self inside and paraded a soft and puerile front. The extent of her real anger determined the extent of deviousness of her guise.

She hated it, but there was no other way. She could affect no balance of anger in her real self with tolerance for narrow people. So she over-tolerated by her high-pitched, strained (pleading?) voice.

****

Here she was at 25, with an over-long list of contrived past experiences.

"You made all your own decisions," her father liked to remind her when she spoke of her lack of pluck. And thus the layers of scaly years, dead as callous skin, blunted her ability to turn the negative to humor. The funniest thing she could think of was frog soup.

The dead scale-void was not limited to occupation/glory. It seeped through to her relationships with others. I.e, there *were* no recent others whose sensibilities she took to. Those who she craved were distant either geographically or in terms of accessibility.

But she'd had enough of Random. Of allowing fate to arrange her meetings with people. No more would she wait for those she craved. Despite her current distaste for the contrived, she lived by the code of Contrived.

She would aggress towards those she craved. Be they people in the public domain (which was how she found out about them most of the time) or be they ghosts of the past whose friendships/souls she missed, she'd get to them.

This plan, along with the writings/music/films of similar anguished beings was her only salvation now.

Chapter 38

She is not galloping or running or skipping or trotting or trouncing or dallying. She is walking on the main street. A very light wind lifts her above the pavement. She cries to herself, "How dare an element of nature--and one that is always a metaphor for freedom--do such a thing to me!" She only wanted to *walk* along the pavement.

Later, after the wind had suspended its hold on her for a while, she returned to her house. She spun her heavy coat down on the floor and hummed a tune, "I-I-I-I-I'm go-ing CRA-zy, catch me if you can..." It had been number one on the AM radio hit parade for over a month, now. She didn't particularly care for it, but it stuck in her throat like a chicken bone.

Frank, a construction worker for Lawrenceville plumbing, who was working on a sewer or water line, said to his coworker Sal, "Hey, there goes that broad again."

"Yep, great rack." Sal spit a piece of phlegm to the curb.

Frank scratched his ass. Sal scratched his balls.

Sally stopped singing and ate an apple. She also wondered where her favorite writer was right now. How was he feeling? She wondered even more than she sat, humiliated, before hundreds of proprietors of companies, Big Men who just might give her a living wage in exchange for servility. She sat and hated them, while exerting all the control she knew over her vocal cords: This voice must come out not harsh, not arrogant, not aggressive or assertive. Her voice came out just barely. It sounded like she was saving it for dessert or something.

One hundred Big Men sat at their collective desk, speaking stereoscopically: "Mmmmm, Hmmmm. Mmmmm. Hmmmm." They stroked their beards or their neatly shaven faces nervously, or at least for lack of anything better to do with their hands. They suppressed their heavy breathing, much as Sally tried to suppress her anger. Their heavy breathing

resisted suppression, though, thus they went into
incoming phone calls, no matter who from, with all
the gusto one would give to one's best friend not
seen for years.

Sally sat, directing the energy not allowed into
Assertiveness to Observation. Her eyes were wide
as they could be without her contact lenses popping
out. She was biting her tongue. If she'd had an
electric wire and plug in place of arms and hands,
all the work of all the ersatz companies would've
been done without the help of any of the workers.
Especially the Bossmen. Sally tried not to stare.
Thus the details she was most expert on related to
inanimate objects of office decor. She was quite
bored on these excursions. She sighed silently.

"Well, we'll certainly call you when something
comes up, Sally. And thanks for stopping by."

Sally thought she should make a recording of
AnyBigMan to spare herself the nausea of having to
hear variations on a euphemism. One looped tape of
one dull rejection was enough. "Ho, ho, ho. What's

that you have there? A tape recorder? Do you always record your interviews?"

"Oh yes, it makes it so much easier to remember the DETAILS," Sally whispered. The BigMens' eyebrows formed an inverted V.

Chapter 39

A composition in blacks and greys

He is busy. He is sooo busy.

She is screaming.

He is busy.

She can hear.

He is busy.

She is screaming.

He is sooo busy.

Some are making music.

Some are making noise.

Few are making music.

He can't hear.

She can hear.

She is screaming.

She has heard music.

She hears noise.

He is making noise.

He can't hear.

He is so busy.

He has not heard music.

He has not heard music.

She is screaming.

She does not make noise.

She can hear.

He can not hear.

He is sooo busy.

Where is music?

When will he hear?

When will he hear music?

When will she stop screaming?

Where is all the music?

Why is all the noise?

Why is he sooo busy?

When will he hear?

He is not you.

She has heard music.

She knows there is you.

He has not heard music.

So few make music.

You do not make noise.

You are screaming.

She hears.

You do not hear.

She is me.

You are you.

You are not he.

You are screaming.

She hears.

She is screaming.

You do not hear.

You are sooo busy.

You do not hear.

You have heard music.

You hear noise.

You make music.

She can hear.

She has heard music.

Most make noise.

Few make music.

You do not hear.

You do not hear.

You are screaming.

She hears.

Most make noise.

She is screaming.

She does not make noise.

You do not hear.

You are sooo busy.

You do not listennnnnnnnnn n n n n n n

n n n n n.

Chapter 40

I may breathe as much as I want. I breathe. I must
stop looking when my boss says so. He will tell me,
"Shut your eyes, now" and I will shut my eyes. He
will tell me to open them eventually, and he will
instruct me to place the glasses with the pink lenses
on the bridge of my nose. He will tell me which
way to point my head: to the left or to the right.
Perhaps he will have me tilt my head upwards,
slightly. Or perhaps downwards, to look at his feet
encased in black spectator shoes with new Neolite
heels. He will tell me when I may eat my lunch and
when I may stop eating it. He will tell me when I
may speak to visitors and when I must remain
silent.

I do as he tells me. I do.

Today it is a Monday. I don't distinguish between
the days "of the week"--as it is called by some--
because I see no way to distinguish. In this spot,
Monday is like Tuesday is like Wednesday is like

Thursday is like Friday is like Saturday is like Sunday is like yesterday is like today is like tomorrow.

I can only distinguish between morning and afternoon and evening, for these are the basic units of time in this spot.

The morning is the time for watching. I may watch more in the morning than in either the afternoon or the evening.

The afternoon is for sitting perfectly still. It is the only period in which this is required of me. I must sit perfectly still. Not even my breathing may interfere with my pose.

The evening is for humming. Contrary to what is ordinarily thought of as humming, humming here is done in one tone, and one tone only. It must be sustained for long periods, often three and four minutes at a take, without the intrusion of breathing. Even though I may breathe as much as I want in the evening, I must confine my breathing to the spaces in between hums. I am not allowed to hum for a shorter take than I am able, for my boss monitors my hums according to my record and keeps a log of all of them, their duration. He knows exactly the length of hums I am capable of producing. If I fail-- and this is not, now, a common occurrence--I am made to repeat the evening before I may have morning.

At first I failed often; at that point, I preferred the watching to humming. But soon my watching was hindered by blinders, which I was instructed to affix to the sides of my head, just above my ears. The blinders pressed into my head and made me feel very sick. As a result, I stopped failing in the evening. I hummed exactly as I was required to.

I have never learned the meaning of certain words that I overhear visitors saying to each other at times. These words mystify me and make me uncomfortable. Some of them are: Paint, wyvern, chocolate, pavid, david, lamb, elbow, civilly, citron, compute, Leda, duck, bigotry, bergamot, potato, pound-foolish and skirt.

I have no way of learning these words, as in the evening, I must hum, in the afternoon I must sit perfectly still, and in the morning I must watch. It is only in the afternoon that the boss occasionally permits me to speak to the visitors. But he only allows me to speak to the visitors whose tongues are foreign. They do not understand my questions. I do not understand their tongues. Invariably, they smile to me. I do not smile to them. I look away, at my feet. My feet are the only area I may watch without instruction. I may watch them at any time during the afternoon. I usually watch them for long periods. When I am watching them, I do not have to watch what my boss instructs me to.

Chapter 41

Maisie and a Visiting Weak-Man

Maisie kept staring at the window, at the dark outside, wishing this visiting weak-man were not here; his pale orange eyebrows, his quickly darting eyes, his baggy trousers. She followed the sidewards glances of his eyes as he pronounced poems. He very pronounced them.

"Stupid!" Maisie was thinking, "You say you don't ever write by speaking into a tape recorder because you can't stand the sound of your voice. Well, what makes you think _I_ feel like hearing it?" Maisie was thinking also that such thoughts were unduly cruel and that she really should try to listen. Oh, but she couldn't stand his timidity. He was like a pale orange fly: it comes into your home uninvited then flies around from fright.

She felt like she could belong nowhere but in the pages of _Ms Magazine_, or maybe, if it were possible, she would like to follow people around invisibly, seeing what their lives were like. A voice then said to her, "But isn't that what *living* is? And each time you are reincarnated, you experience another."

"Oh, but to learn, I'd want to see them all in the same life, comparison-wise." Maisie became all of a sudden a Hershey bar addict.

I am tired of looking for straight up and down handwriting on walls. I am tired of seeing Norman Mailer go on and on in well-fired rhetoric for all these years as I sit and ponder fingers--their number, their length, their texture, their uses, their purpose, the faces whose hands they belong to. I am tired of looking for flying fingers as I walk down Beacon Hill licking a lollipop with a face on each side of it; tired of decorating my mailbox for a mailman who has never even heard of the word "frivolity"; and I am especially disgusted when I find myself sad to hear that an old grammar school classmate/stranger/crush/friend/potential lover is happy living in Brooklyn because he has a lady. Not his ex-wife. An other. I am tired of wondering what pairness is like, chastising my bliss for being uncoupled bliss, biting the inside of my lower lip, all for the elusive, non-existent far-away love. I lick the remaining almonds from between my teeth. The almonds of the eaten Hershey bar.

Maisie opened her eyes very wide, so wide, her contact lenses almost fell out. Oh, what am I to do with all of these unassigned young males who keep tripping on their paths and somehow arrive at my yard? Must I put up a sign "Do not step on the grass"? Must I pretend I am contagious and they will turn into me if they insist on seeing me? Why is it so depressing entertaining the thought of being in the company of, speaking to, looking at, listening to, being looked at by these assorted unassigned guys who find their way to my yard?

Maisie thought hard. She knew not. She sang her newest song, called "The Ersatz Pygmies." Then she smiled and closed her eyes and thought of her far-away soulmate, who was physically, mysteriously ill in England.

Her far-away soulmate

Chapter 42

<u>The Ersatz Pygmies</u>

(a song)

Chorus:

The Ersatz Pygmies are reaching the ford

                reaching the ford

                reaching the ford

                reaching the ford

The Ersatz Pygmies are reaching the ford

                reaching the ford

of the stream.

Pygmies, Pygmies, anywhere
and not a drop to think.

(Chorus:)
I am the water of the stream.
I smile.

I fret.

The pygmies remember

But I haven't been met.

(Chorus again)

I walk the rapids with an asbestos-wrapped enigma

Carefully balanced on my head.

I am doing the model-strut.

But.

(Chorus)

And when the pie was open (as it was)

The Ersatz Pygmies began to sing.

It was an ersatz song.

And I belong

To Donald Barthelme and the ages.

Donald says, "You are lying."

(Chorus)

The Pygmies crawl/up the wall.

They shit on pages of poetry.

They spit on paintings they cannot be.

I am tall.

I am he.

You are there/of/you and me.

There's a pair of knee muscles flexing.

They are drums.

Pygmies are numbs, dumbs.

(Chorus)

The fish are getting kill't.

You are half-kilt.

Our house is almost built.

The wicked witch is dead.

(Chorus)

The Ersatz Pygmies fade.

Everything rushes in to take up their air space.

The winner is your face.

About the Author

Judy Pokras majored in graphic art and design at Pratt Institute, filmmaking at London Film School, and video production at NYU. Judy has worked as a journalist for *The New York Times* and many other publications, both online and in print. She has made videos (like her mock-Seinfeld comedy, *Anomalies*), written raw vegan recipe books, and written and performed songs with her once-upon-a-time NYC band, *Communism*. She wrote *Artist Girl's Cambridge Daze* when she was in her early 20s.

She invites you to "like" this book's Facebook page:

Facebook.com/CambridgeDaze

Made in the USA
Charleston, SC
14 March 2014